EVERETT ANDERSON'S 1 ▪ 2 ▪ 3

EVERETT ANDERSON'S
1 · 2 · 3

by Lucille Clifton

Illustrations by
Ann Grifalconi

Holt, Rinehart and Winston ■ New York

Text copyright © 1977 by Lucille Clifton
Illustrations copyright © 1977 by Ann Grifalconi

All rights reserved, including the right to reproduce
this book or portions thereof in any form.
Published simultaneously in Canada by Holt, Rinehart
and Winston of Canada, Limited.
Printed in the United States of America

10 9 8 7 6 5 4 3 2 1

Library of Congress Cataloging in Publication Data

Clifton, Lucille, 1936-
   Everett Anderson's 1 2 3.

   SUMMARY: As a small boy's mother considers
remarriage, he considers the numbers one, two, and
three—sometimes they're lonely, sometimes crowded,
but sometimes just right.
   [1. Mothers and sons—Fiction. 2. Remarriage—
Fiction. 3. Stories in rhyme] I. Grifalconi, Ann.
II. Title.
PZ83.C573Ew   [E]   76-25866
ISBN 0-03-017441-4

For Darryl, Eric, and Kevin Walker, my friends.   L.C.

To the family of Three I always loved.   A.G.

1

One can eat a whole candy bar alone.
One can win a race.
One can have a drum of his own
or can go someplace
without Mama! One can have fun
alone, says Everett Anderson.

A new someone
has come to stay
and be a neighbor to
14A,
Mr. Tom Perry
who drives a bus.
"He might," Mama says,
"be a friend to us."

1

Everett Anderson thinks that One
is a lonely number.
It's not much fun
talking to yourself all day,
and so he tries to understand the way
that Mr. Perry likes to be
talking to Mama a lot lately.

2

Everett Anderson says, Thank you,
but I have gotten used to Two.
Two at dinner,
Two flying kites,
Two at market,
Two at night, and
I'm not lonely at all, thank you,
I have gotten used to Two.

2

Suppose we stopped being Two?
What would I do?

Everett Anderson worries,
and all the while
Mama keeps smiling
her special smile.

2

"People miss people
when they go.
Everett Anderson,
you must know
I miss your Daddy,"
Mama smiles.

2

"But Two is a lonely
number, too,
sometimes for me and
sometimes for you,
and when things end we
don't just stop,
we keep on being, and
that's the story of
what you're seeing."

3

Everett Anderson's Mama is humming
because Mr. Perry soon is coming.
Sometimes Three is too much to share,
and sometimes Three doesn't fit somewhere,
and Three at dinner crowds the dishes.
Three should be Two! Everett Anderson wishes.

3

Mr. Perry smiles at Everett Anderson's face
and says, "I can't take your Daddy's place,
but I can be me if you'll give me a chance,
and Three can work and sing and dance
and not make a crowd in 14 A."

3

It's still
hard to get used to Three
Everett thinks, but he thinks
he will.

3

One can be lonely and One can be fun, and
Two can be awful or perfect for some, and
Three can be crowded or can be just right or
even too many, you have to decide.

1·2·3

Mr. Perry and Everett Anderson too
know the number you need
is the number for you.